Pickerton's Jiggle

Written by Riya Aarini
Illustrated by Mariana Hnatenko

To those who joyously jiggle
~ RA

Pickerton's Jiggle

Text copyright © 2021 by Riya Aarini
Illustrations copyright © 2021 by Mariana Hnatenko
Book design by Mark Reid, Author Packages

Publisher's Cataloging-in-Publication Data
provided by Five Rainbows Cataloging Services

Names: Aarini, Riya, author. | Hnatenko, Mariana, illustrator.
Title: Pickerton's jiggle / written by Riya Aarini ; illustrated by Mariana Hnatenko.
Description: Chicago : Riya Aarini, 2021. | Also available in audiobook format. | Summary: When Pickerton encounters life's obstacles, he learns to overcome them.
Identifiers: LCCN 2020915082 (print) | ISBN 978-1-7353473-3-2 (hardcover) | ISBN 978-1-7353473-4-9 (paperback) | ISBN 978-1-7353473-5-6 (ebook) | ISBN 978-0-XXXXXX-XX-X (audiobook)
Subjects: LCSH: Picture books for children. | CYAC: Pigs--Fiction. | Self-actualization (Psychology)--Fiction. | Self-esteem--Fiction. | Problem solving--Fiction. | BISAC: JUVENILE FICTION / Animals / Pigs. | JUVENILE FICTION / Social Themes / Self-Esteem & Self-Reliance. | JUVENILE FICTION / Readers / Beginner.
Classification: LCC PZ7.1.A27 Pi 2021 (print) | LCC PZ7.1.A27 (ebook) | DDC [E]--dc23.

Library of Congress Control Number: 2020915082

Visit www.riyapresents.com

Good Pickerton Wickerton
was lively and sweet.
He dared not get dirty.
No pig was as neat!

A small speck of mud
gave rise to a shout.
He'd feel awfully bad
both inside and out.

4

One sunshiny morn, he
rose early from bed,
and these were the first
things he happily said...

"Good morning again,
to bubbly, kind me!
It's you I wake up
each fine day to see.

"Hello, floppy ears
and four wiggly toes.
Welcome, curly tail
and cool, freckled nose.

"I'll give you a scrub
with this bar of soap.
You'll sparkle real soon,
I certainly hope!

"Hello, fine-tooth comb
and black, tangled hair.
For a neat side sweep
there's no better pair."

8

From bottom to top,
no grime could be seen.
Every spot on his skin
was tidy and clean.

Pickerton skipped down
the rickety stairs,
spotless and jolly,
without any cares.

"Well, how do you do,
my rumbling tummy?
These pancakes piled high
sure do smell yummy!"

Gladly expecting
the morning's new day,
Pickerton went on
to excitedly say...

"Hello, morning zing.
I welcome you back!
Surprises await,
as I pack up my sack.

"Whatever this day
brings, gaily I'll sing:
'Oh, greetings, today!
I'm set to begin!'"

Smiling ear to ear,
he stepped off the bus.
He landed in mud
and made a huge fuss!

Splash! Oof! Blubb!

Pickerton's grand smile
flipped upside down.
He stood in the mud
with a big, ol' frown.

His face turned bright red.
Steam blew from his ears.
He faced, all at once,
the worst of his fears!

He was caked in mud
from his head to his feet.
Pickerton fumed as
the sun released heat.

He felt the wet mud
beginning to dry,
then saw he was all right
and let out a sigh.

Because of hard luck,
he wanted to hide,
but he didn't feel
at all bad inside.

He's still Pickerton,
charming as ever.
Will the scum spoil him?
No, never!

BUS
STOP

He started to do
a whimsical wiggle,
then he burst into
a lighthearted giggle.

Smart Pickerton then
shook himself silly,
as all the dry dirt
flew off willy-nilly.

In minutes, the pig
was clean as before.
Not a spot of dirt
was left, not one, no more!

In his special, offbeat,
enjoyable way,
Pickerton went through
the rest of his day.

Whatever befell
young Pickerton,
he turned it into
ridiculous fun.

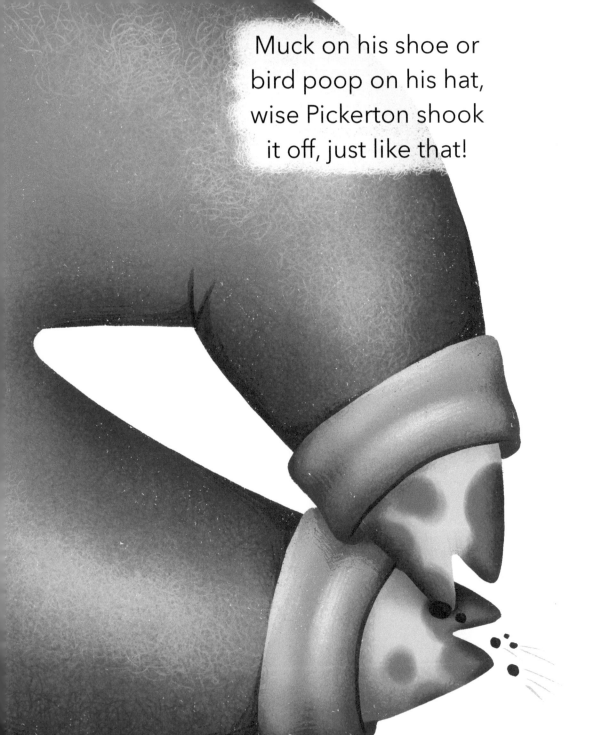

Muck on his shoe or
bird poop on his hat,
wise Pickerton shook
it off, just like that!

There always will be
that troublesome dirt,
and icky bits just
might stick to his shirt.

He soon learned to be
happy as a clam,
and ended the day
the way he began.

He greeted all things
so small and so big
that meant something good
to this joyful pig.

24

Calm Pickerton Wickerton
then closed his brown eyes
and started to say
the day's last goodbyes.

"Nighty night, me,
my very best friend—
whether muddy or clean—
we're friends 'til the end!

26

"Goodnight, wispy hair
bunched high in a heap.
You'll get in a mess
as I go to sleep.

27

It's time to turn out
the bright, glowing light.
And on this clear night,
I'll snuggle down tight."

After one last jiggle,
one just for fun,
the old day was done
for tired Pickerton.

29

Dear Pickerton snoozed,
peacefully snoring,
until tomorrow's
early spring morning,

when he'd cheerily
begin again clean,
as the most particular pig
that's ever been seen.

Thank you for reading *Pickerton's Jiggle*.
If you enjoyed this book, please consider leaving a review, and help other readers find entertaining stories.

Upcoming children's books by this author
The Veggie Patch Bandits
The Enchanting Gingerbread House

Other children's books by this author include
Carefree Ollie series:
Ollie's Backpack (Book One)
Ollie's Haffiness (Book Two)
Ollie's Garden (Book Three)

Stay up to date on new book releases by visiting my author website:
www.riyapresents.com